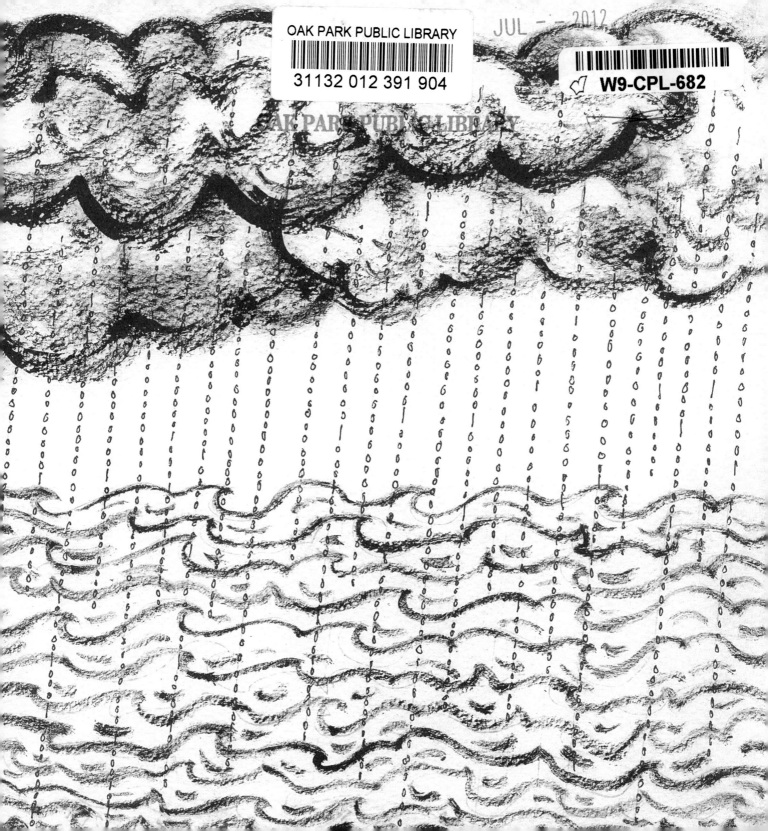

The Flute

For Swami Tejomayananda—RG
To my grandchildren Myna & Vihaan—PB

Text copyright © 2011 Rachna Gilmore Illustrations copyright © 2011 Pulak Biswas
Released in the US in 2012

LIBRARY AND ARCHIVES CANADA CATALOGUING IN PUBLICATION

Gilmore, Rachna, 1953-
  The flute / written by Rachna Gilmore ; illustrated by
Pulak Biswas.

ISBN 978-1-896580-57-9

  I. Biswas, Pulak II. Title.

PS8563.I57F58 2011   C813'.54   C2011-901035-6

CATALOGUING AND PUBLICATION DATA
AVAILABLE FROM THE BRITISH LIBRARY.

BOOK DESIGN BY ELISA GUTIERREZ
The text of this book is set in Triplex and Zapatista
10 9 8 7 6 5 4 3 2 1   Printed in Canada by Friesens Corp.,
Altona, Manitoba in April 2011, on FSG paper using vegetable-based inks.

The publisher thanks the Government of Canada and Canadian Heritage for their financial support through the Canada Council for the Arts, the Canada Book Fund and Livres Canada Books. The publisher also thanks the Government of the Province of British Columbia for the financial support it has given through the Book Publishing Tax Credit program and the British Columbia Arts Council.

FSC
Mixed Sources
Cert no. SW-COC-001271
© 1996 FSC

Canada Council   Conseil des Arts
for the Arts   du Canada

BRITISH
COLUMBIA
ARTS COUNCIL

Rachna Gilmore

The Flute

Illustrated by Pulak Biswas

Tradewind Books

Vancouver ● ● London

Long ago and far away, in a village on the banks of a rushing river, a baby girl was born. The mother cuddled her baby and gazed up at the full moon, glowing in a sky like blue honey.

"Chandra," murmured the mother. "I'll call you Chandra after the moon."

As Chandra grew, she followed her mother like a shadow. Each day she helped her parents in the fields. Each evening she went with them to the banks of the great river. There her mother played her old wooden flute. She played of shimmering hot days and the richness of the earth. She played of the cool evening sky and the growing promise of the moon.

Then one year, disaster struck the village. The monsoon rains came hard and heavy. The river flooded its banks, sweeping away cows, carts and huts.

Chandra's mother pushed her up the tallest tree. "Be strong and hold tight," she cried, then handed Chandra the flute.

Chandra clung to the branch and wept as her mother and father vanished in the flood.

When the waters receded, Chandra returned to her village, a tangle of sticks and mud.

"I suppose I'll have to take you in," said her uncle. He sniffed.

"But you'd better earn your keep," said Chandra's aunt.

Chandra's life now became as cold and hard as before it had been warm and loving. Her aunt and uncle worked her mercilessly. Their two sons tormented her. She became thinner and quieter, fading into a shadow.

But every morning and evening, when she led the cows to the river, Chandra took the wooden flute, worn smooth by her mother's hands. She tried to play of the trees and the sky, but the flute sang only of aching and loss.

At last Chandra's uncle could stand it no longer. He grabbed the flute and flung it into the river. "Stop moaning and get back to work," he shouted.

Chandra rushed to save the flute, but the river swept it away.

It was a harsh and lonely winter for Chandra. She did her best to keep her mother's songs alive by whistling the tunes, but sometimes she couldn't remember them.

The winter was followed by blazing heat. The sun burned and burned, drying the river into a tired trickle. Each day Chandra took the cows further upstream to graze. Crops withered and food became scarce. Chandra was given the least to eat.

One morning Chandra took the cows the furthest they could go. Hunger twisted her stomach. She sank down under a tree. With parched lips she tried to whistle one of her mother's songs.

She could almost hear the sound of her mother's flute.

And then she did hear it. There was no one in sight and yet a flute rang out sweet and clear. It sang of hope and of plenty.

Out of the heat-rippled air, a plantain leaf appeared, laden with rice, lentils and eggplant as her mother used to make.

The food was real! Chandra ate her fill, then slept deeply.

Each day when Chandra took the cows to the river, the flute sang her food, sang her comfort and love.

Each night Chandra's uncle eyed her suspiciously. The cows were skin and bone, yet Chandra's cheeks were filling out. He wondered who could be feeding her.

He sent his older son to follow Chandra.
The boy hid behind a bush. He was
amazed to hear the flute and see the food
appear from nowhere.

When she returned, Chandra was met by her furious aunt and uncle.

"How dare you eat and give us nothing!" screamed her aunt. "Where did you get the food?"

She refused to believe that Chandra didn't know.

"It's unholy magic," said her uncle.

"You're an evil child!" said her aunt. "You must be causing the drought!"

Just then there was a crack of thunder. At last the monsoon had arrived!

In their delight, her aunt and uncle forgot about Chandra.

Rain streamed down all night, and the next day and the next.

The river swelled from a trickle to a torrent, then rushed its banks, eager to swallow the land.

In the pouring rain, the villagers fled to high ground. Chandra tried to follow but her uncle pushed her back. "Keep away, evil one! It's you who brought on this flood."

The water rose quickly. It swirled around Chandra's knees, then her waist, threatening to sweep her away.

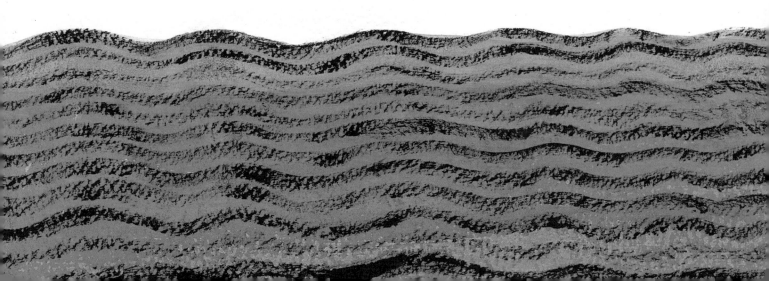

Over the roar of the water, Chandra heard a flute. It was calling from the middle of the river. She hesitated, then struggled deeper into the water. Toward the flute's song. The current rushed her off her feet. The flute trilled long and hard, and something solid swept into Chandra's hand.

It was a rope, tight and strong.

Chandra pulled herself along it, with the flute urging her on.

At last her feet touched ground.

But the rope was gone, and in her hand was her mother's flute!

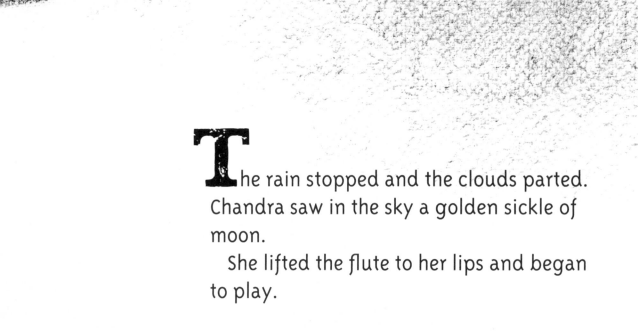

The rain stopped and the clouds parted. Chandra saw in the sky a golden sickle of moon.

She lifted the flute to her lips and began to play.

From out of the shadows stepped a man and a woman.

"Who are you, child?" they asked.

Chandra told them.

"We lost our son in the flood last year," said the woman.

"We used to hear a flute, playing of our loss," said the man. "Tonight we heard it, singing of hope."

The woman smiled. "Will you live with us and be our daughter?"

"Yes," said Chandra. "Yes, I will."

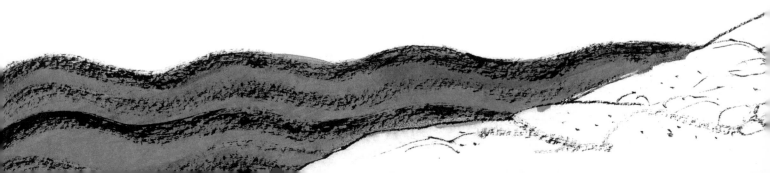

Each day Chandra worked in the fields with her new family. Each evening she went with them to the great river. There she played her flute. Sometimes she played of the day's hot work and the rushing river. Sometimes she played of the darkening sky and the first stars. But always she played of the hope and enduring strength of the moon.

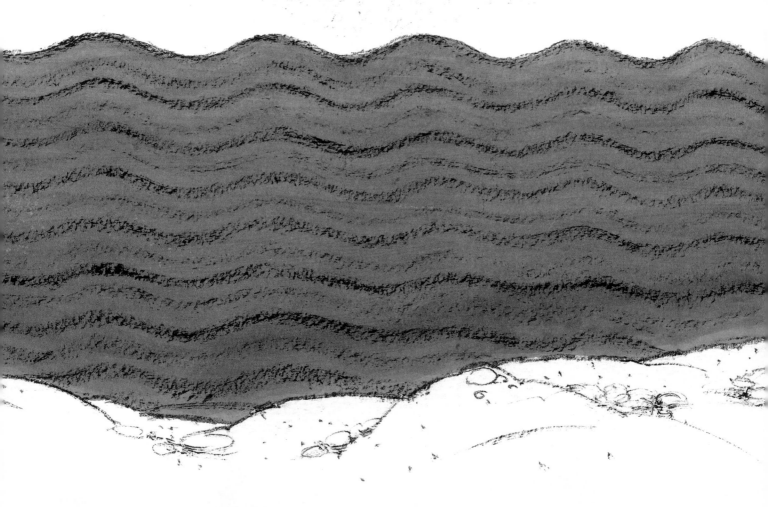
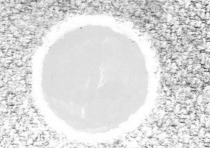